Rise of the Ancient

By Ned Lerr

Based on the Disney Interactive Studios videogame

Original concept by Fil Barlow and Helen Maier

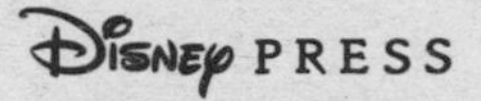

New York

Printed in the United States of America

First Edition
1 3 5 7 9 10 8 6 4 2

Library of Congress Catalog Card Number: 2009923464

ISBN 978-1-4231-0810-8
This book is set in 13-point Sabon.
Visit disneybooks.com

Rise of the Ancient

A long time ago in the Nanairo Galaxy, men roamed the planets in perfect harmony with a rare species known as the Spectrobes: mysterious beings that harnessed light energy to unleash amazing powers. But that harmony would eventually be lost. The Krawl—an evil force that cannot stand light—appeared in the Nanairo Galaxy and wreaked havoc throughout the planets. The Spectrobes jumped into action and the Krawl were finally beaten; but the fight proved too great, even for the Spectrobes. The Spectrobes were fossilized and scattered among many planets where they buried themselves deep in the ground. All was peaceful, but that would not last for long. Deep in the blackness of space, thousands of vortexes filled with Krawl were on their way back to the Nanairo Galaxy. . . .

Chapter One

"Whoa!"

Rallen jumped back just in time. The Krawl's giant tentacle whistled past his head; if Rallen had moved a centimeter less, he'd have lost an ear.

Instead, the Krawl's tentacle slammed into the rocky surface of Genshi. The impact made Rallen stumble. He regained his balance immediately but had to turn his head away as shards of hot, jagged rock thrown up by the force of the blow peppered his face like shrapnel. Rallen blinked rapidly several times, attempting to clear his vision.

Still unable to see clearly, he paused for a fraction of a second. Then, acting on sheer instinct, Rallen blindly dived backward, just as the Krawl's tentacle sliced the air above his nose; the force of the air hitting his face told Rallen that the Krawl had missed him by no more than a few millimeters this time.

Rallen hit the ground hard. With the wind knocked out of him and still unable to see well, Rallen immediately rolled to his right as the creature's massive foot crushed the area he'd just vacated. Instinct was again Rallen's friend, as he quickly leaped to his feet and staggered backward—Genshi was a planet of ceaseless volcanic activity, and although there didn't seem to be any lava in the immediate area, it was always close enough to the surface to make the ground uncomfortably hot. Scalding, in fact.

Rallen inhaled sharply, attempting to catch his breath, but that did almost as much harm as good: Genshi's atmosphere was technically breathable—or so the textbooks on Kollin claimed. But harsh winds that smelled like pure sulfur blew regularly and happened to kick up just as Rallen took in a large lungful of air.

Rallen and his partner, Jeena, had been told by their commanding officer, Commander Grant, to rush to Genshi because the Krawl had been spotted there. That had certainly been accurate. The Krawl—huge, fast, fierce creatures seemingly bent on destroying every bit of life in the planetary system—were here. And under the best of circumstances they were difficult, bordering on impossible, to defeat. Fighting them was a nightmare.

But Rallen knew there were worse nightmares. Losing to the Krawl meant they would go on to devour anything in their path, including entire planets.

"Jeena!" Rallen yelled, or tried to; he discovered his lungs were functioning just well enough for the words to come out louder than a whisper.

It was enough.

"Over here!" his partner yelled from what sounded like about fifteen meters away. Rallen was surprised she'd been able to hear him, but he filed that away for later—now was the time for surviving.

"Water," he called back, slightly louder this time. "I can't see."

"Got it," she replied. "Hold out your hands. I'll— Rallen! Break left!"

Without thinking, Rallen dived to his left, hoping there were no boulders there. He hit the relatively flat ground and continued his shoulder roll, popping up on his feet. To his right, he could hear and feel evidence that he'd just escaped the Krawl's tentacles yet again.

"Hands!" Jeena yelled. Rallen held his hands out in front of him, angled slightly toward what sounded like Jeena's position. He still couldn't open his eyes into more than slits, but a moment later what was unquestionably a Nanairo Planetary Patrol–issued water bottle hit his hands perfectly. He allowed the weight and momentum of the bottle to push his hands down slightly, then pointed the bottle at his face and squeezed.

The water wasn't cool by any stretch, but it was so much less hot than the surrounding air that his body relaxed a bit. More important, it washed away the burning Genshi dust so that he could finally open his eyes.

And not a moment too soon. As Rallen's vision returned, the Krawl he'd been blindly dodging for what seemed like hours sprang into view. Rallen pointed the water bottle at it and, perhaps because it didn't recognize the object, the creature paused. If there was at least one bright side to the situation, it was that the Krawl weren't very intelligent. Rallen took advantage of the extremely brief respite to dive behind a nearby outcropping that had been created by a volcanic eruption at some point in the past.

"You okay?" Jeena called, running up to him.

Part of the outcropping was sheared off as the Krawl's tentacle swung down. "I've, ya know, been better!" he responded.

Rallen looked around for Spikanor and Zozanero, the two evolved Spectrobes he'd brought to Genshi with him and Jeena. He could use some help. And quickly. The dust whipped around by the vortex accompanying the Krawl made it hard to see beyond several feet.

Jeena followed Rallen's gaze and saw that the Spectrobes had their hands—or paws—

full themselves; as amazingly capable as they were, there was only so much they could do. And even at a distance, it was clear that Rallen was going to need help sooner rather than later.

Jeena looked around desperately, hoping to catch sight of something she could use as a weapon—she didn't even have a blaster, and her scientific equipment wasn't going to be of any assistance. Though she was an officer of the Nanairo Planetary Patrol, she was never issued a blaster, for reasons unknown to her. *Maybe there was something else on Genshi that could help?* she thought.

As far as she could see, the entire landscape was nothing but rough igneous rock all the way to the horizon. Throwing rocks wasn't going to be enough.

No. *Throwing* a few rocks wouldn't work. But maybe . . .

"Rallen!" Jeena yelled. "Your Palaceo blaster!"

"What about it?" he cried, dodging several flying tentacles.

"Use it against the Krawl!"

"I left it on the ship!"

"Well, what good is it there?" she cried.

"Jeena! This is *not* the time to argue!" he yelled back.

"Do you have your regular blaster?"

"Come on, Jeena! You know it's no good against these uglies!" Rallen shouted, as another razor-sharp tentacle came crashing down right in front of his feet.

But Jeena had something else in mind. "I know! Go for the ground *underneath* it!"

As the Krawl lifted its whiplike arm again, Rallen surprised the creature by rushing toward it and then jumping clear over its head. He pulled out his blaster in midair and began firing over his shoulder.

The Krawl spun to follow Rallen's progress, but as it took a step, the effects of the blaster started to take hold. The shattered rock began to glow, then gave way as torrents of lava bubbled up through the now-cracked surface. The Krawl stepped back uncertainly, but the ground around it began to shift, and more lava pooled to the surface, slowly covering the monster.

What happened next confused Rallen. The Krawl began to grow.

"Uh, Jeena? Call me crazy, but I think the lava is making this Krawl . . . bigger!"

Jeena, unsure of what to think, took a closer look at the lava-covered Krawl. "It looks like it's combining with the lava," she whispered as lava began flowing through the creature's body.

The Krawl whipped its head from side to side and then, just as fast as it grew, it dissolved. Lava burped up into the air leaving nothing more than a few black spots where the creature once stood.

"Nice shooting, partner," Jeena said as Rallen ran up.

"Yeah, it was," he agreed. Then added with a laugh, "Nice idea."

They watched as Spikanor and Zozanero finished off the four Krawl they'd been fighting. "You know," Jeena commented, "you're awfully good . . . but they're even better. So how come *you're* the Spectrobe Master?"

"Just one of those mysteries," he replied. "And not one I'm unhappy about." Rallen blew at the tip of the blaster and spun it around his finger, sliding it into his holster.

As if alerted by some signal only they could hear, the vortices disappeared, and the Krawl with them. Genshi, even with lava bubbling everywhere, seemed almost peaceful in the sudden silence.

"And without so much as a simple good-bye," Rallen commented, looking up at the red sky.

"Oh, sure, they've been trying to kill us, but does that mean they have to be so rude?"

Jeena smiled wearily. "The Spectrobes do the same thing by popping back into the Prizmod. But I guess it's different, right? Because they're saving your life, rather than trying to take it?"

"Exactly," Rallen agreed, patting the small device on the arm of his suit which somehow could hold the Spectrobes. How was such a thing possible? He'd have to ask Aldous, the old man who'd given it to him. There were so many things about the Spectrobes Rallen still didn't understand. . . .

"Hey, check this out." Jeena knelt down and poked at what looked like a small rock.

Rallen squatted. "What is that?"

"I'm not sure; it looks as if it may be a piece of the Krawl you defeated."

She took out a small container and lightly

scooped some of the strange, charred substance into it. Gently sealing it, she placed the container in her pocket.

"Are you really going to bring that on the ship?" Rallen asked.

"Are you kidding?" Jeena replied. "Of course I am. Maybe this will give us a clue as to what the Krawl are, and how to defeat them."

"Ha!" he shot back. "We already know that: me and the Spectrobes."

Jeena nodded. "Yeah, I'm sure you'd hate to have help."

Rallen didn't reply—unusual for him. This latest encounter with the Krawl was much tougher than he'd have liked. "Still," he said, "I'm not crazy about having even a piece of a stinkin' Krawl on our ship. It's kinda . . . I dunno . . . creepy, isn't it?"

"That's your opinion as a scientist, I take it?" Jeena said, apparently unconcerned. "And speaking of discoveries, it looks like Danawa's found something as well."

They watched as the third Spectrobe who'd made the trip with them, Danawa, began to bounce around. He was always energetic, like all Spectrobes, especially since he was still in Child form. His eyes started to glow, and soon a yellow light poured out of them. Suddenly, he came to a complete standstill, then started jumping up and down repeatedly, making the noises that Rallen and Jeena had previously learned meant he'd found another buried Spectrobe.

"Great," Rallen said. "We get to dig. On Genshi."

"It could be much worse," Jeena pointed out. "You could have to *actually* dig, rather than do it virtually."

Rallen stuck his tongue out at her, then touched the Prizmod. A hologram appeared, showing the location and size of the Spectrobe. A stylus formed in his hand. Rallen used the stylus to make quick strokes on the hologram, scraping away the virtual dirt. As he did, the actual ground by their feet started to move, responding to the movements of Rallen's hand. Soon, an object was revealed.

"And we've got ourselves another fossil," said Jeena.

"Hmm," Rallen said, looking at it. "I guess Aldous will be able to tell us what this one's called."

Jeena picked up the fossilized Spectrobe. "Whew," she said, breathing heavily. "You may be small, but you weigh a ton."

"Hey, you want me to carry him?" Rallen said.

"That's okay." Jeena grunted as they made their way toward the ship. "I think you've done enough heavy lifting for one day."

Chapter Two

The moment the ship broke free from Genshi's atmosphere, Rallen and Jeena both exhaled loudly. The odd timing made Rallen and Jeena laugh. Though they'd only been partnered for a few weeks, it already felt like years.

"Let's get this little guy taken care of, shall we?" Rallen said. He put the fossilized Spectrobe into the incubator that Aldous gave them and which helps the Spectrobes grow. Leaning forward and staring intently, Rallen concentrated.

"Wake up!" he shouted.

The fossil began to shake. Eventually, it exploded with light. The glare was blinding. When Rallen and Jeena were able to open their eyes again, they saw that the fossil had become a real live, breathing Spectrobe. It was longer than it was tall, and looked like a cross between a bird and an airplane. It was more brightly colored than the other Spectrobes they'd met, with blue, red, and yellow feathers covering its body.

"Wow," Jeena said. "She's pretty."

"She?" Rallen asked.

Jeena shrugged. "Who's to say it's not a little gal?"

"I . . . I don't know," he admitted. "Add that to the list of things to ask Aldous when there's time."

"There is time now."

Aldous—the old man who had introduced Rallen and Jeena to the Spectrobes—appeared on the video communicator on the ship's dashboard. The two officers turned around in surprise. Aldous had a way of making an entrance.

"Whoa. Aldous! Long time no see!" Rallen said.

"Yes, Rallen. I am learning much here on your home planet of Kollin. So I hear there are a few things you would like to know."

"Aldous, we found another fossilized Spectrobe, this time on the planet Genshi," Jeena said, pointing to the birdlike creature in the incubator.

Aldous nodded in approval. "Ah, I see you have found Aoi. This Spectrobe is a very special one. It possesses the gift of flight and can sail through the air with excellent speed and skill. When evolved, Aoi will be known as Aoba. Then high-speed air combat will be his specialty. He will be able to use energy stored in his majestic tail."

"So, where I can get some food, er, minerals

to help this little guy evolve?" Rallen asked.

"Young Rallen," Aldous said, smiling. "Always looking ahead. There are a few minerals located under the incubator to get you started. They should hold over the child Spectrobe for a while. That is, until you find more minerals to further its growth."

Rallen pulled a few minerals from under the incubator. One was triangular, another was moonlike, and the third was rectangular. Aoi ate them as fast as Rallen could drop them into the Spectrobe's mouth.

"Hey, Aldous, how long till this little guy evolves and looks like Spikanor or Zozanero?"

"I am not sure. But I think someone else is evolving right now." Aldous nodded to something behind Jeena and Rallen. It was Danawa, and he had gone from standing upright and wobbling to being down on all fours, like a wolf ready to attack. He had quadrupled in size, and his physique looked strong and powerful.

"Oh, my. . ." Jeena said, covering her mouth. "Danawa is so . . . *big!*"

"Ah, he is Danawa no more. Now that he has evolved, you may call him Danapix. He can emit huge shock waves, perfect for long-range attacks. He is a strong ally to have on your side. Well, if you'll excuse me, I have to meet Commander Grant and continue filling him in on this new threat we are facing. Jeena, Rallen, good luck." And with that, the monitor went black.

Jeena pointed to the young Komainu, still in its Child form, as it rubbed up against her leg. Since he was one of the first Spectrobes Jeena had met, she'd grown quite attached to him. "Don't worry! Your time will come."

"A Komanoto, huh? Ah, they grow up so fast," Rallen said, sounding like a proud parent. "So, what planet should we go save now?" he said, putting his feet up on the ship's dashboard.

Jeena put her head back and tapped her chin. "I've heard Himuro is nice this time of year."

"Sounds good to me," Rallen said, with a yawn. "I feel like I haven't had a day off in months."

"I know," Jeena agreed. "Hard to believe it's only been a few days, isn't it?" Rallen looked at her in surprise.

"Seriously? Is that really all it's been?" Rallen exclaimed.

Jeena nodded. "It's been"—she checked the ship's clock—"fifty-two hours and nineteen minutes since we saw our first Krawl."

"Man . . . no wonder I'm so tired," Rallen said, yawning. "And speaking of, you guys should get some rest, too." He held up the Prizmod and the Spectrobes knew it was a signal to jump in.

But after thinking for a moment, he took Zozanero back out. "I think he might have worked himself a little too hard back there. Those

Krawl sure gave him a lickin'. I'm going to let him stretch for a bit."

"You know, we've got a while to go until we get back to headquarters." Jeena locked in the course and triple-checked their location. "I'm going to run a few quick tests on that bit of dried-up Krawl back there. You can grab a quick nap if you want."

"I dunno," Rallen replied, closing his eyes. "Maybe I'll just rest for a minute."

Within seconds, his breathing had slowed. Jeena smiled. She was pretty wiped out, too—the past few days had seemed like weeks, and it felt as though she hadn't had a good rest in a month. But scientific curiosity was getting the better of her—exhausted as she was, she couldn't wait to see what she could find out about the Krawl.

This was her best chance to find out what the creature was made of, its chemical composition. Maybe she could even start sequencing its DNA. She was excited about the simple act of *discovering*, but she also wanted to make sure it was safe to bring to NPP headquarters.

Jeena pulled on one of the airtight suits that were stored on board the ship. She glanced over at Rallen, who was snoring gently in the copilot's seat. Each area of the ship, small as it was, had its own atmospheric controls, and she'd set the filters so that Rallen would be in a virtual air lock with his own oxygen supply. Jeena knew that with this extra precaution, there would be little chance of him being exposed to anything airborne should the worst happen.

After preparing an examination area on a flat surface she'd sterilized, Jeena carefully opened the evidence container and laid out a piece of the Krawl's remains. She inspected it under the ship's microscope—it wasn't nearly as good as her lab's, but it would do in a pinch.

As far as she could tell from her rudimentary

tests, the thing was completely safe, and there should be no danger in transferring it to her lab at headquarters.

As one last extrathorough test, Jeena attached a small electrode to the remains, wondering if she would get any type of reading at all. She rather doubted it, but she figured many scientific discoveries occurred just because scientists wondered, "what would happen if . . . ?" She flipped the switch, looking at the monitor.

Then, out the corner of her eye, Jeena saw something move, causing her to turn her head. When she realized what was happening, she gasped. The Krawl was regenerating! The small sample was already ten times the size it had been seconds before, and it was still growing. Jeena cut the power to the small electrodes, but the Krawl was still getting larger.

She looked around for a weapon. Unfortunately, there was nothing on hand more threatening than a scalpel, and she knew from experience that wouldn't do much good. Why hadn't she grabbed a blaster before she started? Even in her fear, of course, she knew the answer: she was a scientist, not a soldier.

Then something else caught her eye. Jeena realized a Spectrobe—Zozanero—was standing next to her. But he wasn't growling or threatening to attack. He was waiting for a Spectrobe Master to give him a command. And while she was many things, Jeena was no Spectrobe Master.

"Rallen!" she cried. But between her protective suit and the air lock separating them, there was no chance of him hearing her.

Jeena knew it wouldn't be much longer. Although only seconds had passed, the Krawl was already so large it couldn't stand up straight inside the ship. Refusing to go without a fight, Jeena grabbed a scalpel and threw it at the Krawl, hitting it exactly in the midsection, and to Jeena's surprise, the instrument disappeared *into* the creature. Suddenly, a large blade began to develop where one the Krawl's tentacles used to be.

It combines with whatever it comes in contact with! she said to herself.

Before Jeena could make another move, the Krawl lunged for her.

"No!" she cried, closing her eyes.

The next thing she knew, she was sitting down. What had happened? Had the Krawl knocked her backward? And why were her ears ringing?

And more importantly, where was the Krawl?

She looked around, utterly bewildered. The ship wasn't large; there was nowhere for the Krawl to hide. And yet all she could see were bits of ash on the floor.

Jeena turned around to see Rallen standing by his chair, his hair still mussed from sleeping.

"I can't leave you alone for a minute, can I?" He grinned, shaking his head.

He stepped forward and reached out a hand to help her up, but Jeena ignored it, getting up by herself. "You know," he continued, "most people think Grant put us together so you could keep an eye on me. But I always suspected it was the other way around."

Rallen holstered his Palaceo blaster, then walked over to the large ash pile and poked it with a boot. "Wow. Really did a number on him, huh? He must not have been fully regenerated. And did you notice that when you threw that scalpel at it, it just seemed to become a part of it?"

"Yeah," Jeena said quietly. "I just had first-hand experience."

He turned around to Jeena and said, "Although, if that was the case, then why did the lava on Genshi seem to kill it? Maybe too much lava? But what's too much lava? I mean . . ." Rallen stopped talking. He noticed something was off with his partner. "Jeena, what's wrong?"

Jeena turned away. "Nothing. I'm fine."

Rallen paused. It was clear even to him that his partner *wasn't* fine. "Oh," he said, not knowing what else to say.

Still facing away from him, Jeena shook her head. "I'm sorry," she said. "I just . . . it was so dumb of me. I should have taken extra precautions. She paused. "And I thought . . . I mean, you were asleep, so I thought you wouldn't even know. And the Krawl . . . it would be my fault."

"Oh," Rallen said again. Then he laughed. "Is *that* all? Oh, jeez. Wow. That's really nice and everything, to, you know, care about me like that. But, hey, seriously, don't give that a second thought."

Jeena turned to look at him in amazement. "What?"

"Well, you know," he said, "it's not like we're, I dunno, accountants or something. This is a dangerous job, and we picked it, right? I mean, I knew what I was getting into when I applied to the Nanairo Planetary Patrol. Didn't you?"

She stared at her partner. Then, to her surprise, she laughed. "Well, no, not exactly—I mean, I certainly had no idea I'd be facing the Krawl. For that matter, I had no idea something like the Krawl even existed. But you're right—I knew the NPP could be dangerous. And dealing with the Krawl can prove difficult when you're not a Spectrobe Master, especially at times like this. But . . . seriously? You're not mad at me for . . . you know . . . ?"

"Almost destroying the ship while I took a nap?" Rallen said.

"Yeah, that," Jeena said, looking down.

"Nah. Now, if you'd totally destroyed it, rather than almost, maybe I would be upset. But maybe not, since I wouldn't really be around anymore. So, how long till we're planetside?"

Jeena shook her head. She was getting much better at reading her partner, but the jumps he made in conversation still threw her sometimes. "Well . . . it looks like we should be back in about twenty minutes."

"Awesome," Rallen said, stretching out again. "Just enough time for a few more quick *z*'s."

As Jeena, Rallen, and the Spectrobes left the ship, Maxx, the chief mechanic, dropped her jaw in awe. Peering inside, she let out a bark. "Whoa! What did you do to my ship?"

Jeena tried to decide how to respond. "You wouldn't believe it," she finally said.

"Oh, yeah?" Maxx growled. "Try me."

"A fight to the death with a previously

unknown alien life-form," Rallen called over his shoulder as he walked away.

"Yeah, right," Maxx said.

"Told you!" Rallen called, breaking into a run.

Maxx shook her head, looking at the ship's interior. "Actually . . . I almost *could* believe that."

"And that brings us up to date, sir," Jeena said as she finished her report.

"Hmm," Commander Grant murmured. Rallen and Jeena waited patiently. They'd learned that their commanding officer was not to be rushed; his style tended to be slow and steady, calm and collected.

Suddenly, his eyes bore down on them. "You're both to grab some chow," he said, "then I want you to head for the natural-science museum. There's an astroarchaeologist there, Professor Kate, who just might be able to give you . . . a new perspective on this incredible threat we're facing."

"Right," Rallen replied. "Food—lots of food—and then we'll meet the scientist. Jeena, ever met this Professor Kate?"

"I've never met her. I've just heard about her. Her studies are kind of . . . well, a big deal. In the scientific community," she added, looking at Rallen's skeptical expression.

"If you say so." He shrugged. "But right now, I'm way more interested in the perspective a double traxburger can give me."

Jeena pulled out a test tube with the Krawl sample in it. "Could we get the lab to run a diagnostic on this sample we picked up while on Genshi? I have a feeling there is a lot more to learn."

Commander Grant stared at the sample. In fact, he couldn't peel his eyes away. Jeena and Rallen both noticed and shrugged to each other, unsure of what to make of Commander Grant's sudden strange behavior.

"Uh, Commander?" Rallen finally said.

Blinking several times, Grant broke out of his daze.

"Yes. I'll . . . I'll take this sample to the lab," he said. Then he grabbed the vial from Jeena and walked out of the room.

"What was that all about?" Jeena asked after the commander had gone.

"I don't know. It's like he had seen that sample before or something . . . Okay. Food. I need food," Rallen said, running to the cafeteria.

Jeena shook her head and chased after him.

Chapter Three

"Hello. I am Dr. Webster, the curator of the museum."

Rallen and Jeena stuck out their hands. "Hey, how you doing?" Rallen said. "I'm—"

"Late," interrupted Dr. Webster, spinning away. He was standing on an individualized hovercraft, and Jeena and Rallen had to break into a trot to catch up with him. As soon as they pulled alongside him, Dr. Webster increased his own speed slightly, moving just fast enough that walking at top speed wasn't quite enough, but slow enough that jogging was too fast, forcing Rallen and Jeena to go back and forth between the two.

"Sorry," Rallen said, although he didn't sound like he meant it. "We didn't get our orders until today. And we weren't told that getting here by a specific time was a matter of life or death."

Jeena noticed that Dr. Webster had been looking at them out of the corners of his eyes as they trotted along on either side of him. He had a barely perceptible smile on his face at first, but as he turned to glare at Rallen, any sign of amusement was gone.

"Listen, you young whelp," Dr. Webster said, his voice high and brisk. "There are literally dozens of things I could be doing with my time, any one of which would not only be more interesting and pleasant, but which would have a distinctly beneficial result for me. Instead, I am to play nursemaid to a pair of ingrates who have not the slightest comprehension of where they are or—"

"The Museum of Natural Science on the planet Kollin," Jeena said softly, "designed by the great Iline Merie. The largest and most prestigious museum in the entire Nanairo Galaxy, it houses the remains of approximately seven hundred and eighty-six thousand now-extinct species, including the Grairo, the Ninex, and the Hyferug, as well as the deadly Steenpring. Recently acquired several specimens long believed to be extinct, such as the—"

"You have made your point," Dr. Webster said. He wasn't smiling . . . but he wasn't glaring anymore either. "I suppose I should not be entirely surprised, given your own lineage. Shall we proceed? Professor Kate must be nearly through with her lecture by now."

Rallen looked at Jeena quizzically, but there was no time for questions, as the doctor turned a corner abruptly. They continued down one corridor after another, each one tantalizing Jeena with a glimpse at the museum's seemingly never-ending collection of fascinating specimens . . . and boring Rallen, who only saw a seemingly interchangeable collection of stuff.

Finally they stopped outside a lecture hall. "I assume you can be trusted to sit quietly during an academic talk?" Dr. Webster asked, then he turned and hovered off without waiting for an answer.

Rallen stuck out his tongue at the retreating figure. "Thus proving his point," Jeena said. She couldn't help feeling thoroughly annoyed both by the curator, for his arrogant attitude . . . and by Rallen, for giving Dr. Webster some justification to behave that way.

They opened the door as quietly as they could

and snuck into the back row. Standing on a stage at the front of the auditorium was a tall woman with long hair.

Rallen decided that as long as he was going to be stuck there anyway, he may as well listen, but within a minute he gave up. He counted the number of people in the audience—the place wasn't even a quarter full. Then he closed his eyes and tried to sleep.

Jeena, on the other hand, was utterly entranced. She couldn't take her eyes off the slides Professor Kate was putting up: gems, minerals, and sketches of sites, even what appeared to be actual drawings made by something the professor called only "The Ancients."

All too soon, the presentation came to a conclusion. Jeena was frustrated that they'd heard so little of Professor Kate's talk. At least, she thought, there was going to be a question-and-answer period.

Sure enough, Professor Kate asked if there were any questions. There was a low rumbling that ran through the crowd, but no one said anything. Jeena was confused. She had two dozen questions that came to mind immediately. How could none of the other attendees have anything to ask?

Finally, one of them, a thin fellow with short green hair stood up. "I just want to be quite sure I am understanding the thrust of your main theory," he said slowly. Professor Kate waited silently. "You are claiming that the ruins on the planet Nessa are actually the remains of some sort of ancient machine, an ancient *spacecraft*? Created by some ancient peoples you've named, appropriately enough, The Ancients. Is that essentially it?"

Professor Kate nodded. "That is what the evidence I have been presenting for the past two hours has led me to conclude, yes."

The man scoffed, not even bothering to hide

his disdain. "Preposterous. I cannot believe I just wasted my time on this balderdash." He grabbed his hat and cane and hobbled out of the auditorium.

Jeena's mouth fell open in shock. Surely he would be shouted down by the others.

Instead, the rest of the audience stood and walked out as well, some laughing, some with angry expressions, many checking their kaylees. In a minute, Professor Kate, Rallen, and Jeena were the only ones left.

At the front of the room, Professor Kate methodically gathered her things. Jeena hastily pushed past Rallen, causing him to snort and sit up abruptly. "I was just going to—Mom!" he said, then shook his head. "Oh. Is it over already?"

Jeena hurried down to the front of the auditorium, with Rallen close behind. "Professor?"

Professor Kate looked up with a tired but pleasant expression on her face. "Yes? What can I help you with?"

"Well, I had a few questions. Several, actually," Jeena said, laughing.

"Mmm. Allow me to guess. Your first question is, am I insane? Your next is, does someone actually pay me for this nonsense? Your third is . . . I'm not sure what your third is. How *do* you get a refund, perhaps?"

Jeena waved her hands frantically. "No! No, not at all. I was just wondering if you thought the spacecraft had, in fact, been used for intergalactic travel or was merely a design. Is there any chance that it landed there from *another* planet? Or another galaxy? Or another dimension? Or perhaps—" Jeena broke off in midsentence. "What's wrong?" she asked, responding to the odd look on Professor Kate's face.

"I'm sorry, it's . . . it's just that I'm trying to figure out if you're pulling my leg or not."

Jeena blinked. "Why would I be kidding?"

Professor Kate laughed. "Ah, a girl after my

own heart. I take it you're a scientist, too?"

"Oh, no!" Jeena responded, and then to Rallen's surprise, she seemed to blush. "I . . . I mean, yes, but . . . no, not like you. I mean . . ." Her stammering trailed off.

"Wow," Rallen said admiringly. Then, turning toward the professor, he added, "I don't really have, well, pretty much any idea who you are—but anyone who can stump Jeena like that is okay in my book."

Professor Kate smiled and held out her hand. "Well, I must say, between her scientific inquisitiveness and your honesty, the two of you are the most pleasant pair I've encountered today. I'm Professor Kate."

Rallen shook her hand. "Pleasure. I'm Rallen, and my tongue-tied partner here is Jeena. We're here to ask you about something but, uh . . . I wasn't really paying much attention so I can't tell you what."

"It's about the ruins on Nessa," Jeena responded, apparently determined to regain her composure. "Commander Grant of the Nanairo Planetary Patrol believes they might shed some light on a recent . . . discovery of ours."

Professor Kate grew serious. "Really? Commander Grant? Interesting. What kind of discovery? Did you stumble across a previously unknown archaeological site? Or some fossils?"

Rallen and Jeena looked at each other. "Well . . . I guess you could put it that way," Jeena said.

"Although they tend to move a lot quicker than most fossils—from what little I know of fossils, of course," Rallen said.

Jeena noticed the skeptical expression returning to the professor's face and hastily added, "It's a long story."

"Mmm," the scientist murmured noncommittally. "Well, as much as I'd like to hear it, I'm afraid I've got to be returning to Nessa. So if you'll excuse me—"

"Actually," Jeena said, "if you don't mind, we were hoping to accompany you back to the dig. We'd very much like to see the site—"

"We would?" Rallen interjected.

"And," Jeena continued, elbowing Rallen in the ribs, "that'll give us an opportunity to introduce you to our . . . fossils."

"Introduce?" Professor Kate asked.

Rallen shrugged. "Like she said, it's a *long* story."

"Hey, is that the site?" Rallen asked, pointing at one of the monitors.

Professor Kate seemed to have trouble tearing her eyes away from Zozanero, who was clearly smitten with the scientist. He'd had his head in her lap from virtually the moment she boarded the ship. He was heavy—*very* heavy—but

Professor Kate didn't object at all. . . . Although she hadn't been capable of speech for the first ten minutes after meeting the Spectrobes anyway.

"Uh . . . yes," she said finally. "Yes, that's the main site we're working on now."

"Huh," the pilot said. "Looks pretty cool from up here. Where do you want me to put her down?"

"If you don't mind walking a little, the western face would be best—it offers the least chance of disturbing any of the more sensitive areas."

The ship banked steeply but smoothly. Moments later, they touched down so gently that Professor Kate was unaware they were on solid ground.

Chapter Four

Professor Kate wasn't even fazed by the hike from the ship to the ruins, a trip over steep and rugged terrain that Rallen swore had been designed to be as inaccessible to humans as possible. The sand sucked at their boots, and the ground was littered with rocks of various sizes—all the way up to boulders you had to navigate around—making walking difficult.

"Well, this is it," Professor Kate said, as they crested the final ridge and came around a corner.

There before them lay the ruins. Pride was all over the professor's face. Jeena's eyes glittered. The pyramids lay partially uncovered, but somehow you got the impression that there was at least as much underneath the ground as there was above it. Even Rallen had to confess there was something about the site that somehow resonated inside him.

"It's incredible," Jeena said breathily. Then, catching herself, she shot a glance at Rallen. Her face hardened; she obviously expected him to tease her about her fan-girl tendencies.

Instead, he just nodded. "Yeah, this really is pretty cool." He grinned. "I mean, considering it's, you know, a big pile of rocks and sand in a desert where adults can dig like little kids."

Professor Kate laughed. "I suppose that's one way of looking at it."

The professor led them into a large cavern. "Here, let me show you where we first discovered the artifacts that led us to suspect there was a significant find here," she said.

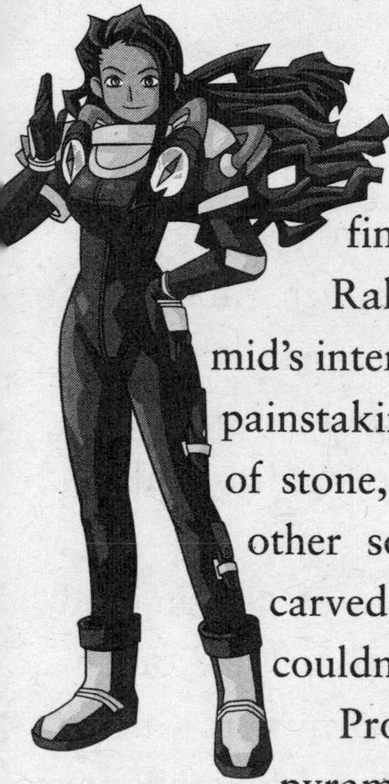

Rallen caught sight of the pyramid's interior. The idea that someone had painstakingly cut these enormous blocks of stone, stacked them on top of each other so they fit perfectly, and then carved ornate runes into them . . . he couldn't wrap his head around it.

Professor Kate led them into the pyramid. The passages twisted and turned, and it was not rare for the team to come across other passages that broke off from the main corridor. Sometimes Professor Kate took one of these other passages, and sometimes she didn't. It occurred to both Rallen and Jeena that there was no chance they'd ever be able to find their way back to the surface without the professor as their guide. Rallen shivered. He lived for the unfettered freedom of space, of being able to go in any direction at any time, the thrill of speed. It didn't seem to bother the Spectrobes, who were still bounding around with as much enthusiasm as ever and appeared able to see fine without the aid of much light, but Rallen couldn't imagine a worse way to die than underground in a dark, cramped place.

Professor Kate looked over at Rallen and saw him shiver a bit. "The temperature differential between the surface and down here can be pretty extreme. We've been going downhill for nearly a half mile now, but we'll be climbing soon, and that'll warm you up. Once we reach the stream, the path will curve back up."

Professor Kate sped up slightly so she could go through a particularly narrow section first.

As she did, an odd crevice in the cave wall caught Jeena's eye. It was almost perfectly round. She was just about to ask Professor Kate if it had had some importance to the daily living of the Ancients when the scientist suddenly screamed.

Professor Kate stumbled, catching her heel on an outcropping of rock. The noise startled Jeena, and she leaped up immediately, instinctively reaching out and catching the scientist just before she fell.

Rallen had somehow gotten in front of the group, despite the fact that he'd been bringing up the rear until that point. His laser sword was in his hand, and the Spectrobes were on either side of him, growling and waiting for a command.

"No! Please! Don't!"

The voice that rang out was so obviously full of fear that Rallen took a step backward—although he didn't put away his laser sword yet. The Spectrobes didn't move, but their growling quieted.

Professor Kate moved forward. "Who are

you?" she demanded, any trace of shock now erased.

A man stepped forward, his hands in front of his face to block the light coming from the professor's flashlight. "It's Sekou, from the village. We worked together on the excavation."

The scientist's brows creased. "Sekou? Of course, I remember you. But what are you doing here?"

The man stepped forward hesitantly. He was tall and thin, with long yellow hair. He didn't seem to be any sort of threat, but his very appearance was so odd that they were all on guard.

What he said next, however, chilled their blood.

"We didn't know where else to go. When those . . . those . . . *things* . . . came, we just ran."

Rallen and Jeena looked at each other. "What things?" Jeena asked softly.

Sekou shook his head. "I don't know how to

describe them. I've never seen their like before. You're going to find this hard to believe, but this enormous whirlwind appeared out of nowhere and these huge creatures with these tentacles for arms—" He broke off, his voice choked with horror.

Professor Kate stepped forward. "It's all right. We believe you."

Sekou looked up. "You . . . you do?"

"Unfortunately, we've met your new friends before," Rallen replied.

"Hold on," Jeena said, tilting her head to one side. "You said 'we ran.' Who were you talking about?"

"Oh," Sekou responded. "Well, all of us."

He stepped back and made a sweeping gesture with his arm. Rallen, Jeena, and Professor Kate peered through a narrow opening. The beam of the professor's flashlight showed at least twenty people behind Sekou.

"Whoa," Jeena said. "It's suddenly turned into quite the party down here. We're going to need to—"

"Is . . . is that a Prizmod?" Sekou asked suddenly, staring at Rallen's gauntlet.

Rallen looked confused. "How do you know what a Prizmod is?"

Sekou's eyes grew dark. "That is a somewhat lengthy tale." He straightened up and raised his chin. "But one you should know—you are a Spectrobe Master, are you not?" Jeena and Rallen looked at each other.

"Spectrobes are not unknown to us," Sekou explained. "Long, long ago, a number of Spectrobe Masters lived on Nessa—our planet was, in fact, one of their main bases. There were many battles between the Spectrobes and the eaters of light, battles which could last weeks, even months—or so the legends say."

"What else do the legends say?" Rallen asked.

Sekou looked intensely at Rallen. "They say that these *Krawl* finally had victory nearly in hand. The Spectrobes and their Masters were valiant, but the Krawl's numbers were simply overwhelming. Until, that is, the Ultimate Form appeared."

"Ultimate Form?" Jeena said.

Rallen nodded. "Aldous mentioned something about that. But . . . what is it?"

Sekou shook his head. "We do not know. Much information was lost over the years." He continued, "After the release of the Ultimate Form, the Krawl were eradicated from our system. But victory came at a heavy price: the Spectrobes were fossilized as a result of the debilitating battle and scattered to the surrounding planets and galaxies."

"For safety," Rallen said.

"Precisely. It was believed that it would be harder for the Krawl to eradicate the Spectrobes entirely were they not all in one place. But the Krawl did not return, and the Ancients lived long in peace and harmony."

"Didn't return until *now*," Jeena said.

"Yes," Sekou agreed.

"Sekou," Professor Kate said, "why did you never tell me this?"

The man smiled. "Would you have believed me?" The scientist didn't answer. "Perhaps you would have. But would anyone have believed you?"

Professor Kate snorted. "Not a chance."

Sekou spread his hands. "Well, there—you see. Besides, although I had heard many of these stories as a child, I was never sure if they were history or myth. It was only when I began to study the markings on the walls here in the ruins that I started to suspect the truth behind the legends. Even so, I was not prepared for just how horrible the Krawl really are."

The others all nodded.

"I'm not sure it's possible to be prepared for that," Jeena said.

Rallen started to respond, then noticed Sekou was still staring at him. "What?"

"The wall said you would come," Sekou said.

Rallen blinked. "Excuse me?"

"The wall said, 'The devourers of light known as the Krawl will one day return, and when they do, a new master will be born.' *You* are that master."

There was a heavy silence in the cave, until Jeena said, "Did the wall say anything about when he'd stop taking his boots off on the flight back to NPP? Because I gotta say, it gets pretty toxic sometimes."

Rallen gave Jeena a grateful look. He could tell she was simply attempting to lighten the mood, and he appreciated it. As cool as it was to be a Spectrobe Master—and it was—the pressure could be pretty crushing. And finding out he was the subject of some ancient prophecy certainly wasn't helping.

Something occurred to Rallen. "Huh," he said. "I've been wondering why the Prizmod fits so perfectly into my suit."

"Maybe Commander Grant knows more than he's let on," Jeena suggested.

"I get the feeling that Grant and I will have a lot to talk about when we get back to NPP headquarters," Rallen replied. "Okay. So . . . what do we do?"

Professor Kate had been staring between her feet at the floor of the cavern during most of the story. Now she looked up. "Well, we have to get them out of here, obviously."

Rallen rolled his eyes. "Well, yeah, I got that. It's not like we can let them stay down here."

"No, no," the professor replied. "I mean away

from this area completely. In fact, I think we should get them off Nessa."

"Whoa," Rallen said. "That's pretty extreme. I mean, I guess it's not a bad idea . . . but how? Our ship can't come close to holding this many people."

"Rallen's right," Jeena agreed. "But . . . maybe we can call for backup. If there's an NPP supply ship in this quadrant, we might be able to get authorization for them to provide a pickup."

Professor Kate nodded. "That would be wonderful, obviously. I'm no expert on NPP protocol, but isn't that highly unusual? Is there any chance you'll get clearance?"

Rallen waved a hand dismissively. "Clearance *schmearance*. I know one of the freighter pilots, Fay Roamenk—she and I were in the academy together. I can probably—"

"I'll call Commander Grant when we get to

the surface," Jeena interrupted. "You're right, this *is* highly unusual. But we've been running into a lot of highly unusual things lately," Jeena said. "I have a feeling the commander will be okay with this one breach of protocol."

Commander Grant had a local supply ship detour to Nessa immediately. Rallen and the Spectrobes were on high alert for any sign of the Krawl. With his Palaceo in one hand and Spikanor and Zozanero on either side of him, the Spectrobes and their master were ready for anything. But the rescue ship entered Nessa's atmosphere before any danger arrived. Assisted by the ship's crew, Jeena and Professor Kate helped the refugees to board.

"That everyone?" one of the crew members asked, after the last of the villagers had boarded.

"Huh," Professor Kate said, scratching her head. "I did a count down in the dig, and I thought we had one more. I must have miscounted in the dark."

Jeena pointed. "Or maybe not."

They peered under the ship. On the other side, they could see two pairs of human legs—one apparently belonging to a small boy, the other quite clearly to an officer of the Nanairo Planetary Patrol. Bounding back and forth between them were two very happy Spectrobes.

"Uh, Rallen?" Jeena called sweetly. "If it's not too much trouble, could you perhaps finish up your game now so these traumatized people can get away from the scene of their terror?"

"What's that?" Rallen called back. "Oh. Oh! Right. Sorry. The Spectrobes and I were just having a quick game of gabb tag with . . ." He looked at the boy. "What's your name anyway, buddy?"

The little boy smiled. "Smurray."

"Well, okay. I'm afraid it's time for you to go

to Kollin with the rest of the folks."

Smurray's smile dimmed. "Are you coming?"

Rallen laughed. "No, we've gotta go someplace else. We're on a big-deal mission, see?"

The boy's eyes glittered. "Really? A mission? Can I come?"

Rallen shook his head. "Sorry, pal. Official persons only." The boy's expression grew sad. Rallen knelt down on one knee and said, "Wouldn't your mom be lonely without you?"

Smurray was quiet, then whispered, "I dunno. I guess. Maybe."

"Rallen," Jeena called.

Rallen didn't look away from the boy. "What's up?"

"We just heard from Commander Grant again. The Krawl have been spotted heading back toward Genshi." Jeena tone was soft but urgent.

"Great."

"But that's not all. He said that there was

something else with the Krawl. Some mysterious . . . being."

Rallen looked up, held his breath for a moment, and then exhaled. "I hear you." He sighed, then turned back to Smurray. "Listen, buddy, we really have to go. I'm sorry, but it's urgent. We have to go, and so do you."

Smurray looked down at the ground with a fierce scowl. "Fine. Go."

Rallen gently took the boy's chin and made him look up. "Tell you what, Smur. When I get back to Kollin, I'll come find you first thing, 'kay?"

Smurray stared into Rallen's eyes. "You promise?"

Rallen squinted. "I promise."

He helped the boy onto the freighter and gave the "all clear" sign. As the hatch started to close, Smurray ran forward. Rallen started to yell a warning, but before he could, the boy called out, "Rallen?"

"What?" he called back through the shrinking gap.

"Are you gonna stop them? Are you gonna stop the Krawl?"

Rallen grinned. "Oh, yeah. *Big*-time."

Smurray gave Rallen a thumbs-up and stepped back, disappearing into the ship just before the hatch sealed. A minute later, the ship took off. Rallen watched it until it disappeared, then turned to Jeena and Professor Kate.

"Let's do this thing," he said.

CHAPTER FIVE

"Ah, Genshi. Oh, how I've missed you." Rallen banked the craft smoothly, and the lava-encrusted surface filled the portside monitors.

Jeena snorted.

"Am I missing something?" Professor Kate said.

"No one who's not on Genshi is missing something," Jeena said. "I don't know if you've ever been here before, but it's not the most pleasant of locations."

Professor Kate shrugged. "It certainly could smell better, and a nice cool breeze once in a while would be delightful. But it's fascinating from a geological point of view.

Rallen craned his neck to look at her. "Are you serious?"

She nodded. "I am. It's clearly not perfect for human habitation, but from a scientific standpoint, it's a gold mine. Metaphorically speaking."

Rallen and Jeena looked at each other. "Well," Jeena said.

"Learn something new every day," he responded. "Or, lately, every hour."

"But," Professor Kate added, "when it comes to one's comfort level, the place really does stink."

"And yet you insisted upon joining us," Jeena pointed out.

"I did," the professor admitted. "Unpleasant atmosphere or not, the adventure this little trip promised was of the sort no self-respecting scientist could possibly turn down."

Professor Kate glanced over at Jeena to see if she understood.

Jeena looked around quizzically, then quickly pulled out her kaylee. Although it was far from unusual for her to use her handheld computer, the intensity of her actions was disturbing.

"What's the problem?" Rallen asked.

"Nothing—and that's the problem," she replied. "There's nothing here but us and lava, both molten and solid."

"Right," said Rallen slowly. *"And?"*

Jeena looked up at him. "And where are the Krawl?"

Rallen's brow furrowed, and he looked around uncertainly. "Huh. You're right. That is kinda weird. Still, no Krawl is good Krawl, right?"

"Not necessarily. What if . . . I don't know . . . what if they're headed somewhere else right now?

And that place is completely defenseless because we went to the wrong planet?" Jeena spoke faster and faster, working her kaylee at a speed Rallen had never seen before. "Or what if—"

Rallen looked at his partner's wide eyes and put a hand on her shoulder. "Jeena. No. There's just no way. Look, I'm sure—"

An explosion not five meters away blew Rallen and Jeena to the ground. Rallen scrambled to his feet and stood in front of Jeena, ready to protect his partner. He looked up through the haze of dust and debris and saw that it hadn't been an explosion—it was the now-familiar whirlwind of a vortex.

The Krawl had arrived.

Rallen took a step back. This time, the Krawl looked different. They were still, well, Krawlish, but now they were mainly red and yellow and orange and . . . and were they . . . were they *molten*? Rallen couldn't be sure, but it looked as if they had adapted to the lava that seemed to be everywhere. "Can they *do* that?" Rallen muttered. "It doesn't seem fair."

The blast had knocked Professor Kate back against the ship. Her mouth was open and her eyes widened at she stared at the tornado which had dropped from the sky with no warning. Dark, nebulous shadows had begun to emerge. The professor couldn't make out any details, but there was something so utterly alien about the creatures that even with molten lava bubbling nearby, her skin broke out in goose bumps.

"Hey, don't worry about it," Rallen called over to her. "We've got this covered!"

He activated the Prizmod and his laser sword and stepped forward, displaying more confidence than he felt. Sure, he'd

done battle with the Krawl a half dozen times already. But he'd been pushed to his limits each time. And he knew that with an enemy so quick and powerful, it would take only one misstep to ensure he'd never fight again.

Rallen decided to have Danapix battle alongside Spikanor and Zozanero, now that Danapix had evolved into his Adult form.

"All right, Spikanor," he said. "You show Danapix the ropes—the Krawl may have evolved somehow, but hopefully so have we, right?"

He moved forward. "And let's try to make sure that none of us come out of this the worse for wear. In fact, let's just make sure we all come out of this."

Spikanor and Zozanero flanked Rallen, as usual, while Danapix took a position right in front of Rallen. They all moved forward together, cautiously. Slowly, five giant menaces covered in bubbly lava emerged from the dark. "And there they are. What do you say?" Rallen asked his comrades. "Let's do this. *Iku ze*!"

The moment the Spectrobes heard Rallen's battle cry, they leaped forward. Rallen rushed ahead as quickly as he could, heading directly for the center Krawl. It brought one of its enormous tentacles down like a sledgehammer, and when it made impact, lava exploded from the ground. Rallen ran low between the feet of the Krawl, slashing with his laser sword as he went. But he had to use much more force than usual to cut through. This Krawl's lava-encrusted exoskeleton is so much tougher than before, he thought . . . but it *could* be done. Eventually, the Krawl bellowed and dropped to its knees.

"That's one!" called Rallen. He looked over to see Spikanor jump and knock into a different

Krawl, driving it into a pool of bubbling lava. Suddenly, the Krawl that fell into the pool burst out. It had almost doubled in size and was now making its way toward Rallen.

Rallen strained his neck looking up at the massive lava-covered Krawl. "Uh, guys," he said, looking around for the Spectrobes. "I could use a little help he—" Before Rallen could finish, the Lava Krawl blasted three fireballs straight at him. Due to his thorough training at the NPP, Rallen was able to dodge them just in the nick of time. But before he could regain his fighting stance, three more fireballs were on their way. This time Rallen wasn't quick enough. He closed his eyes and braced for impact.

"Huh?" he said, opening his eyes.

When the smoke cleared, there stood Danapix, unharmed. The new Spectrobe turned to the Lava Krawl, cocked his head back, lifted his front legs, and stomped them back down to the ground, creating a shock wave. The shock wave crashed into the Krawl and knocked it through the air.

But there was yet another Krawl making its way toward Rallen. He tried to circle around behind it, but the Krawl was too fast and easily kept pace with him. The heat and the smoke from Genshi's environment were beginning to get to Rallen, and he suddenly realized he was on the verge of exhaustion.

The Krawl seemed to sense its advantage and began pressing toward Rallen, driving him further and further back. Finally, there was nowhere left for Rallen to go. He was up against a large stone outcropping, and there were rivers of bubbling lava to either side of him. Suddenly, the Krawl's mouth—or what looked like its mouth—began to open. A blast of fire shot straight for Rallen. Again, his instincts kicked in, and in the blink of an eye, Rallen sprang straight into the air, with only the soles of his boots getting slightly burned from the blast.

That was close, Rallen said to himself. He waited until the Krawl raised its tentacle to strike another crushing blow, then blindly leaped backward. His feet landed on the small ledge of the rock wall behind him just as the tentacle whistled past his face. He immediately sprang into the air again. At the apex of his jump, he was even with the top of the Krawl. He slashed with his laser sword as hard as he could. The Krawl hit the ground a mere second after Rallen landed again. Jeena came running over.

"You okay?" Jeena asked softly, putting a hand on Rallen's shoulder. He looked up at her through the strands of hair falling over his eyes. He tried to blow the hair out of the way but didn't have enough breath. Jeena chuckled softly and brushed the hair away for him, but he could see that she was troubled by his physical state.

"Rallen . . ." she said tentatively. "What *was* that thing?"

He shook his head wearily. "It was big, strong, fast, smart, and scary—and it was covered in molten lava. Beyond that, how should I know?"

"Hey, you're the Spectrobe Master, remember?" Jeena replied.

"Is that right?" he responded, and his grin, though tired-looking, was reassuring. "I almost forgot. Well, what I do know is that that new Spectrobe, Danapix, is something else! Did you see that shock wave rip the Krawl in half?"

Jeena's eyes widened. "Yeah! Aren't you glad he's on our side?"

"Every day I wake up," Rallen said jokingly.

Professor Kate approached tentatively. "So, uh . . . that's, uh . . . that's the Krawl, huh? You know," she said, looking around, "I'm beginning to reconsider my love of fieldwork. A nice, quiet, sterile, *safe* laboratory environment is starting to look awfully good right now. . . ."

"I hear you on that," Jeena agreed. She walked around the ship, inspecting it carefully.

The professor watched. "Anything wrong?"

Jeena brushed some soot off one of the exhaust ports. "We've been riding her awfully hard these past few days, and going from one extreme environment to the next isn't the best way to treat her."

They boarded the ship, the Spectrobes boarding last.

Jeena and Rallen ran through the preflight checklist, and the ship seemed in good working order, although one thruster seemed a little cranky. "It probably got a little bit of debris in it when we landed," Rallen suggested. "A few stray bits of volcanic dust might've been kicked up. When we get out into the vacuum of space, that should clear right out."

As Rallen promised, things got much

smoother once they broke free of Genshi's atmosphere. Professor Kate didn't know whether that was because there was absolutely no weather in space to push the ship this way and that, or because Rallen had been right about the vacuum of space clearing out any debris. Nor did she care. Things got easier. After the past hour, that was the only thing that mattered to her.

She thought maybe she'd just close her eyes for a minute. Just to rest them a little. And with that, Professor Kate was sound asleep.

Chapter Six

"Fighting monsters really takes it out of you, huh?"

Professor Kate struggled to open her eyes. It felt like someone had put a weight on each eyelid. "Hmm?" was all she was able to murmur.

Rallen's laughter startled her, and her eyes shot open. The memory of the past few hours came rushing back, and she was as wide awake as she'd ever been in her life.

Jeena nodded sympathetically. "We can relate.

The Krawl take some getting used to."

"Yeah," Rallen agreed. "Hey, professor, we're just about to break Nessa's atmosphere."

Professor Kate took in the view; she loved her studies, but there was still nothing quite like the view of the universe from space.

There was silence on the ship. Everyone was in their own world as the ship sailed across the galaxy.

Suddenly the ship shuddered; then it began to roll slightly. "Storm?" Jeena asked, snapping out of her trance.

Rallen looked grim. "Nope. Perfect weather. Looks like the debris stuck inside the thruster cleared out after all. Hang on, guys. This might get a little bumpy."

Jeena and Professor Kate held on.

Rather than staying on a direct course, Rallen let the ship guide him. When he felt it gliding one way or pushing in another, he went with it, before slowly coaxing it back into roughly the direction of the dig.

"Where are we?" Jeena asked.

"Uh . . . that'd be Nessa," Rallen responded pointing to a small circle on the dashboard monitor.

Jeena rolled her eyes. "I was looking for something a little more specific. Professor?"

The professor looked at the monitors. "Wow, we're quite a ways from the dig. I haven't been to this part of the planet very often. I think this section is called the Counsel Flats. Why?"

Jeena shrugged.

Rallen swung the ship back toward their original destination. "Home again, home again, jiggety-jig," he said as they came in for a landing. "Always nice to be home again, huh, prof—"

He broke off as the ship made a noise none of them had ever heard before, almost like an asthmatic cough. It shook and dropped for the final few meters, in contrast to the silky smooth landings Rallen was known for.

"It wasn't me!" he said quickly, as they unbuckled and headed for the door. Once outside, they walked around the ship. Rallen grumbled—when it came to flying, he liked challenges . . . but not ones that might involve damage to his ship.

Jeena, on the other hand, looked concerned, even a bit sad. "Are you all right?" Professor Kate asked.

Jeena laughed softly. "I'm fine. I'm sure I'm just being silly. It's simply . . . this ship has gotten us out of more than a few tight spots. And I guess . . . well, I feel bad that we've been so hard on her, that we pushed her to this point. I know," she said, holding up a hand. "It's not our fault. We did all we could under the circumstances. But I still feel bad."

"Yeah, well," Rallen said, walking up to the damaged thruster, "we may just have a more serious problem than nostalgia. I don't think she's up to making another interstellar trip. We're going to have to call for a rescue.

"Jeena?" Rallen continued. "Would you make the call?"

Jeena nodded. She realized the call might sound better coming from her instead of Rallen.

She expected to be reprimanded by the commander for pushing the spacecraft so hard. To her surprise, Commander Grant replied, "I'll have a team fly a replacement craft out to you immediately."

Jeena relayed the information.

"Great," Rallen said. "You just *know* whoever's bringing us the new ship is going to hide a booby trap inside."

The others stared at him. "What?" Jeena asked, astonished. "Why do you think they'd do something like that?"

Rallen shrugged. "Because I would."

With time to kill, they decided to get out of the sun and finish the tour of the ruins they'd aborted earlier.

When they reached the place where they had been surprised by the villagers, Jeena remembered her earlier question. "Oh, I wanted to ask . . ." Jeena began. Then she paused.

"Yes?" Professor Kate said.

"Well," said Jeena, "I was going to ask what the little circle cut in the wall down there was for. But now I just noticed there's another one." She pointed.

Professor Kate was silent. Then she slowly reached out and touched the hole. She pointed her flashlight at it. The hole wasn't very wide, but it was impossible to tell how deep it was.

"Hey, there's a third one up there," Rallen said, pointing his own light at something higher up.

They all stood back, noticing how the three

circles aligned. Any one of them could have just been an indentation in the rock—a natural occurrence. And they were far enough apart from each other that it was easy to overlook the lowest one or the highest one. When one saw all three lined up, there was no question that they'd been very carefully designed.

"Wait a second . . ." Professor Kate said. Then she ran off into the darkness. Rallen and Jeena looked at each other.

"I ain't stayin' here without her," Rallen said.

Without even bothering to reply, Jeena hurried after the scientist.

Professor Kate was kneeling down, searching through a chest filled with what appeared to Rallen and Jeena to be a bunch of rocks. "Couldn't be . . . could it?" the professor muttered. Suddenly, her hand shot up, grasping what looked like a large egg. A moment later, she reached in and grabbed another, then she turned and rushed back to the previous chamber. Rallen and Jeena followed.

"Shine your light on that, would you?" the professor asked. Rallen and Jeena both illuminated the middle hole. Professor Kate slowly, carefully took a dusty green stone egg and slid it into the hole in the wall.

It didn't fit.

"Oh," she said, deflating. "Well, that's disappointing. The idea that we'd found a secret lock that a combination of keys could—"

"What about trying another one?" Rallen asked. "How about that one?"

The professor smiled indulgently. It seemed as if she was embarrassed by her earlier excitement and didn't want to point out how unlikely this all was. And, sure enough, the other rock egg—this one a pale pink—didn't fit either.

"Huh," Rallen said.

"Try them in the other slots," Jeena suggested.

Professor Kate squatted down, and carefully tried the green egg on the lowest opening. Nothing. Sighing, she tried the pink.

It slid in perfectly.

"Dude," murmured Rallen. The others nodded.

Professor Kate stood on tiptoe and tried to fit the remaining key into the upper slot. This time it, too, slid in perfectly.

"Well," she said, standing up.

"Okay. So. We've got three locks and two keys," Jeena said. "We need to find the third."

Professor Kate shook her head. "No. These two were found on a sort of shelf in a small room off the main chamber near the entrance. There was some thought at the time that they might mean something, so we searched high and low for others. But we never found any. If the third stone still exists, it could be anywhere—except where we found the first two."

They fell silent. "Jeez," Rallen finally mumbled.

"It could be crushed, or it could have fallen into the underground stream or been stolen—I mean, who knows how long it's been since . . . what?"

"That's it," said Professor Kate softly. Then she beamed. "That's it!"

"What's it?" Rallen asked, looking around.

Professor Kate was looking off into the distance, clearly trying to remember something—although the way her foot kept jiggling indicated how excited she was. "There was this guy a while back who came to the museum. He said he'd come into possession of a colored egg of some sort. He said he got it from a dig . . . on Nessa! He wouldn't given any more information about it, and I thought he was just trying to con me."

"Do you remember his name?" Jeena asked.

"I . . . think so. . . . Yes, I do. He tried several times to get an appointment. Cyrus. His name was Cyrus. And if I recall correctly, he's got a mining operation right here on Nessa."

"Well," said Rallen, "It looks like I'm going to go see Cyrus—but I'm not calling ahead for an appointment."

By the time Rallen, Jeena, and Professor Kate got back to the surface, their replacement ship was arriving. Commander Grant had ordered a pair of patrol ships to rendezvous on Nessa, and then one of the crews was going to have to hitch a ride back with the other. This didn't make either crew happy.

"I sure hope we're not inconveniencing you," said one of the patrol-ship pilots to the crew they'd be riding home with.

"Nope," the other pilot replied. "*You're* not inconveniencing us at all." They both turned to stare at Rallen.

Rallen rolled his eyes. "Yeah, fellas, that's right. I made sure my ship bit the dust just to be a hassle."

"From what I've heard, it wouldn't surprise me," muttered the first pilot. "Let's get out of here."

Rallen waved at them cheerfully until they were out of sight. He entered the replacement ship and looked around. "Careful, fellas," he said to the Spectrobes that followed him. "Who knows what kind of goodies they left us."

But he didn't see anything amiss, and he didn't have time to waste. He sat down—or was about to, when something made him stop. He looked down . . . and saw he was about to sit on a piece of gum. "Very nice," he said. The copilot had left his ID behind. "Well lookie here." Rallen smiled as he used it to scrape off the gum.

Cyrus wasn't hard to find. Rallen contacted Commander Grant, who gave him everything they had on Cyrus—which wasn't much. The only thing known for sure was where he could be located. But, that was enough for Rallen.

The mining operation was visible from a long

way off. Tall steel beams rose from the ground, and hammerlike oars swung behind them. Large trucks went in and out of a nearby mountain carrying tons of dirt and rock to nearby dumping grounds. Rallen set the ship down in an open area and he and Zozanero went out to investigate. Night had fallen, and bright lights were set up all around the perimeter of the operation, casting shadows everywhere.

A tall man with blond hair came out of what appeared to be an office building and quickly walked up to them. "Hello," he said, reaching out to shake Rallen's hand. "You must be Ranin."

"Rallen," he corrected automatically. "Cyrus?"

"Welcome. Nice to see you. And your . . . dog?" Cyrus looked at the Spectrobe dubiously. "Can I get you something to eat or drink?"

"Thank you," Rallen said. "But we really don't have time to chat. I just need the egg-shaped stone you spoke to Professor Kate about a while back."

"Of course. The stone! I'd be pleased to. Absolutely." Cyrus smirked.

"Great," Rallen said. They looked at each for a few seconds. Cyrus didn't seem to be in any hurry to actually go retrieve the key. "Uh . . ." Rallen finally said, unsure of how to proceed. "So . . . if you'll just give it to me . . ."

Cyrus smirked. "Give it to you? Why would I do that?"

"Well you told Professor Kate about it . . . and . . ."

"I did, indeed I did. And I'd be quite happy to hand it over to you. Just as soon as you give me a diamond mineral."

Rallen blinked. "Diamond mineral? What . . . what's that?"

"As the name implies, it's a mineral, and it's rare. I need it for . . . well, never mind that,"

Cyrus said, waving a hand. "I simply need it. You get it for me, I give you the stone. Everyone wins."

Rallen sighed. "Fine. Where do I get a diamond mineral?"

Cyrus laughed. "Why, on Genshi, of course!"

Rallen rubbed his forehead. "Of course."

As Rallen's ship took off, a flash of movement caught his eye, and he turned to see a large, dark shape running away. Had Rallen brought someone with him? The idea disturbed Cyrus. But, he decided, what's done is done. Besides, the figure was moving away from him—if it had been *approaching* that quickly, *then* he'd be worried.

"Hmmph," Cyrus grunted. "Shadows."

Chapter Seven

If Genshi looked ominous during the day, at night it was positively terrifying. The lava on the planet's surface gave off an eerie glow, and a strange light poured through cracks in Genshi's crust. The occasional volcano eruption stood out starkly against the dark night sky. "Good times, right, buddy?" Rallen asked Spikanor. The Spectrobe merely looked at him.

Rallen found a dark patch and decided that probably meant it was one of the safer places to land. He jumped down to the planet's surface and began looking for the telltale signs Jeena had told him would indicate the presence of the diamond mineral.

There, off to the right, across a small stream of lava, was a faint rainbow. Jeena mentioned that at night the light from the lava would be refracted through the diamond mineral like a prism. Once again, she'd been correct. And so was Komainu, who was jumping up and down, yelping in the direction of the diamond mineral.

"You'd better stay here, pal," Rallen said to Spikanor. "I don't think there are any Krawl around, and I don't want stray lava eruptions to catch you. Oh, and watch the little guy," he said, pointing to Komainu, who had climbed onto Spikanor's back. Spikanor turned and gave Komainu a slight nuzzle with the tip of his nose. He was in good hands.

Rallen got a running start and jumped over a

lava stream. He landed far on the other side, having jumped much farther than was really necessary. This was definitely a case of "better safe than sorry."

The diamond mineral seemed easy enough to acquire—he simply had to break through a small crust of volcanic rock in order to reach in and grab it.

Or so it seemed. He pulled his hand back instinctively. There was no lava visible, but the heat in the small pocket around the diamond mineral was intense. Rallen blew on his fingers to cool them. Well, he thought, what choice do I have?

"None" he said aloud, jamming his hand down and immediately closing his fingers on the diamond mineral before his autonomic reflexes could force his arm to jerk back. Rallen dropped the diamond mineral, which was nearly as hot as the rest of the small crevice, and blew on his hand again. Then he scooped the diamond mineral into a small pouch he'd brought and turned to head back for the ship. A light caught his eye, and he looked at his arm, surprised. The Prizmod was glowing. And Rallen knew that could only mean one thing.

"Krawl?"

"Well done," a dark figure hissed.

Rallen drew his laser sword. He didn't know what this thing was—it was no Krawl—but it was large, much larger than he was. It was so dark around the figure that Rallen couldn't make out details of its features, but it seemed to be wearing a dark cloak. And it was on the planet Genshi, where he knew from experience, no creature in its right mind would go to.

"Who are you?" Rallen demanded. "What do you want?"

The creature simply hissed.

"You're not getting the diamond mineral," Rallen said defiantly.

"What use do we have for that?" the creature responded.

Rallen was confused. If it didn't want the diamond mineral . . . what else could it want?

"We want the Spectrobe Master," said the creature.

Rallen didn't need to hear any more. He sprang forward, slashing with his laser sword. The creature stepped back smoothly, pivoted, and began forcing Rallen backward toward a stream of lava. With no running start, it was going to be a much more difficult to leap over the lava this time.

In desperation, Rallen screamed and made like he was going to rush the creature. To his surprise, it flinched. That was the opening Rallen needed. He turned and ran, diving over the lava. He rolled to his feet and without checking to see whether the creature was following or not, slashed at the edge of the rock with the sword. The ground gave way, and lava spouted high in the air. Suddenly the stream of lava was like a geyser.

"In!" Rallen yelled to Spikanor and Komainu as he ran past, and the three of them jumped aboard the ship together. Moments later, they were airborne.

Rallen pounded on Cyrus's door. Then, without waiting for an answer, he opened it and stormed in.

The office looked normal, but there was no sign of its occupant. "Hello?" Rallen called, his anger rapidly cooling. "Cyrus?"

Rallen noticed an open door off to one side and peered into it. Inside was a set of stairs, but they went down so far that Rallen couldn't see the bottom.

"Hello?"

Rallen spun around to see Cyrus approaching from the back of the building. His voice sounded quite a bit older than during their first visit.

Cyrus closed the door firmly. Rallen felt a pang of guilt for walking into the office. Then he remembered Genshi, and his anger returned.

"I got the diamond mineral," he said curtly.

The smile returned to Cyrus's face. "You did? Oh, that's delightful!" He held out his hand.

Rallen didn't move. "There was an entity there who didn't seem to want me to get it."

Cyrus shrugged. "Well, as I said, it's quite rare."

"He seemed to know I was coming," Rallen retorted.

Cyrus could sense Rallen's anger, but he shook his head in confusion. "Is that so? Well, I had nothing to do with that. After all, I *wanted* you to get me the diamond mineral."

Rallen looked down. It was true, that

wouldn't have made much sense. He held out the diamond mineral.

Cyrus reached for it, but Rallen pulled it back. "The stone," he said.

The strange man snapped his fingers, then reached into a pocket and produced a stone egg very much like the others they'd found, although this one was blue. Unlike the other two key stones, which were each a dim, dusty hue, this one was polished to reveal a gorgeous azure tint. They each held out their objects and made the exchange all at once.

Rallen turned to go, but he paused at the door. "Where did you get the key?"

"What key?" Cyrus asked.

"The one I'm holding," Rallen said, exasperated.

"The stone? How should I know where that came from?" Cyrus replied. "You're the one holding it."

Chapter Eight

Rallen, Jeena, and Professor Kate each held a key stone; they'd polished the first two and discovered that what seemed to be a pair of old rocks were actually stunning works of art, gleaming with color. "Let's do this at the same time. Ready?" the professor said. The others nodded. "Well, then . . . On the count of three: one . . . two . . . *three*!"

Each of them slid their key stone into its slot at the exact same moment. Then they all paused and held their breath.

Nothing happened.

"Oh, you *gotta* be kidding me!" Rallen burst out. "After everything—"

Suddenly, his voice was drowned out by a thunderous noise that kept getting louder and louder.

"What *is* that?" Jeena yelled over the din.

Professor Kate cocked her head. "It's . . . it's water!"

"Is it the underground stream?" Jeena shouted.

"I don't know!" the professor replied. "There shouldn't be nearly enough water here to make that loud a sound. Unless . . . we somehow triggered a flood."

They all looked at each other, eyes wide. If the ruins started flooding, would they be able to reach the surface quickly enough to avoid drowning?

The professor rushed toward the sound. "What are you doing?" Rallen called.

"My job," she called over her shoulder. "I'm going to investigate."

"Oh, boy," Jeena said, following.

"They're crazy, you know that?" Rallen said to the Spectrobes. "I know, I know—who am I to talk? Let's go."

Rallen quickly caught up to the others. They were standing at the edge of the stream, looking down. Rallen peered down as well. Instead of the flooding they'd feared, the water was disappearing, rapidly and loudly.

"Whoa," he said. "It just keeps going."

Finally, there was nothing left except a now-empty riverbed . . . and a door.

"That could be it," whispered Professor Kate. "The final clue to finding the ancient machine's control room."

Jeena nodded. "This could prove you were right about the Ancients."

"Whoa," said Rallen. "Are you saying that

this might be the entrance to some ancient ship's cockpit? I am so there. Now. How do we decide who's going? Rock, paper, scissors?"

"There is no way I'm *not* going down there," Professor Kate quickly replied.

"No," Jeena responded. "Unfortunately, he's right. At least one of us has to stay up here in case something goes wrong. We need to let people know what's happened. Honestly, professor, you really shouldn't be the first one down."

"Why not?" the professor asked. Her eyes were full of nothing but storm clouds now.

"Because," Jeena answered frankly, "neither of us will be able to find our way out of here to go for help if something goes wrong."

Professor Kate looked frustrated. "I hate it when someone very logically tells me why I can't do what I want to do." She narrowed her eyes at them, then put one hand behind her back. "Ready? One, two, three . . . *shoot*!"

* * *

"I still think you cheated," Jeena said.

"How do you cheat at rock, paper, scissors?" Rallen asked.

"I don't know. If I *knew*," she added, breaking into a grin, "I'd be the one going down there and not you."

Rallen laughed. "Tell you what. I'll cut you in for at least five percent of what I find down there."

"Whoa, what?" said Professor Kate.

"Oh, don't worry," he said. "You'll get five percent, too."

Professor Kate began to splutter.

"Fine, fine," he said. "Ten percent. But that's my final offer. See you both soon—with fame and fortune." With the Spectrobes in the Prizmod, Rallen headed for the door.

Climbing down into the dry riverbed was more difficult than it looked. It was uneven and lined with large stalagmites that previously had been hidden by the water. And once Rallen made it across the riverbed, he had to climb up the other side, which took some doing.

"I could sure use Dr. Webster's hovercraft about now," he said, pulling himself up on the ledge.

Rallen found himself standing in front of a door with no lock or handle. "Not even a bell," he said aloud to himself.

He pushed the door, but it wouldn't budge. He tried to get his fingers into the cracks around the doorjam, but they were too narrow. Then he noticed three holes off to one side, arranged in a triangular pattern. "Ah," he said. "I might have just the thing."

He pulled out the key stones; he'd brought them with him at the suggestion of Professor Kate, despite his own initial concerns that removing them might cause the water to come rushing back. But it hadn't, which they took as confirmation that the keys might be needed on Rallen's quest.

As soon as he inserted the stones, the door pivoted open. And when he pulled them out, the door stayed open. Rallen shone his flashlight through the door, but could see only a ramp leading down into darkness.

"Jeena, you reading me?" Rallen said into his wrist communicator.

"Loud and clear." Jeena replied. "Everything okay?"

"Yeah. So far so good."

Rallen cautiously took a step.

"Well," Rallen said, "here goes nothing."

"Good luck," Jeena replied. "Keep in touch."

And with that, Rallen was out of sight.

"That Rallen sure likes adventure," Professor Kate said.

Jeena smirked. "Yeah. Sometimes I envy him."

"Because of the action? Or because he's a

Spectrobe Master?" Professor Kate asked.

Jeena was caught off guard. She'd never really thought about it. "Well, I mean it must be fun to be, you know, a Spectrobe Master. But the responsibility and all . . . I mean, I'm not saying I couldn't handle it, but . . ." Jeena searched for the words to tie together her sudden rant.

"But what?" Professor Kate crossed her arms and waited for Jeena's reply.

Jeena sighed. "I'm just a scientist for the NPP. Rallen's the Spectrobe Master."

Professor Kate nodded. "Fair enough. But wouldn't it be exciting to be a Spectrobe Master?"

Jeena stared at Komainu, who was busy running in circles. "Yeah. It would be cool. . . ."

Rallen continued to walk down the path, slowly and carefully. Suddenly, he heard sand beginning to pour in, though that didn't automatically put him on alert. Instead, he scanned the area with his flashlight, trying to locate the source of the sound. Suddenly, strange purple lights began to glow, illuminating the room.

Rallen could see he was in a large round chamber, which was rapidly filling with sand. Almost as soon as he'd processed this, he saw black smoke begin to pour in as well. *Great*, he thought. *I get a choice of being buried in sand or suffocated by smoke.*

Instead, Rallen chose a third option. He sprinted forward, then dived over a rapidly growing sand dune below the smoke cloud. He sprang to his feet and looked down to see he'd landed on a circular platform made of enormous stone blocks. Had he gone a few more meters, he'd have fallen into an abyss.

Before he had to time to think about what to do next, the center of the platform began to glow with an odd green light. Then, the entire platform shot up with such velocity that Rallen's knees buckled.

It eventually came to a sudden halt, and Rallen found himself in another chamber. Fortunately, this one didn't seem to have any sand or smoke. *At least not yet*, he thought. *Give it time.*

A ramp connected his platform to the rest of the chamber. He tested it with one foot and it seemed solid, so he walked across it as quickly—and gently—as he could.

"Jeena, you there?" he said into his communicator.

There was no answer.

"Figures. Well, not the first time I've been on my own." He'd pretty much always been a loner—he hadn't ever had many close friends. In fact, the only person he'd ever really been close to was his mother. He pushed the thought of her away. This was no time to get lost in memories.

The main section of the chamber had three large circular areas carved into the floor. "Man,"

Rallen muttered, "whoever built this place sure liked the number *three*."

Each circle had a hole right in the center.

Rallen grabbed one of the key stones at random, which turned out to be the pink one. He held it over the hole, then paused. For reasons unclear even to himself, he decided to try the green one first. When he held it over the hole, the patterns around the hole began to glow a pale green. And when the key stone was inserted, the patterns became luminous. "Well, that's helpful," he said.

Rallen inserted the pink key stone next, and then he paused. What was going to happen when the final key stone was inserted? "Well," he said, "I guess we won't know until we try."

Rallen slipped the third and last key stone into place. Instantly, colorful beams of energy shot toward the roof of the chamber—and kept going. Suddenly, his Prizmod began to glow a bright white.

"Whoa," he said softly, then jumped when Jeena's voice was suddenly in his ear.

"Rallen?!"

"Jeena! Hey!"

"I take it you're alive," Jeena said. "When the ground opened up, we were worried. What are you doing down there?"

Rallen laughed. "Long story. I'll fill you in later. For now, let's just say I think the good professor's got her proof."

Jeena laughed, too, and Rallen was pleased to hear how relieved she sounded. "I think you're right," she said. "And you know what else? I know this is crazy, but . . . I think we might be able to fly this thing."

"Wow," Rallen said. "After what we've been through lately, I keep thinking there's nothing crazier that can happen. And yet, there you go."

Chapter Nine

"Base, this is . . ." Jeena paused. "This is Ancient One, requesting clearance for landing. In fact, I'm requesting three clearances—this bird is a bit on the big side."

"Ancient One?" came a voice over the comm. "Who is . . . Jeena? Is that you?"

"Affirmative," she replied.

"What are you . . . who or what is Ancient One? What has that partner of yours done to you?"

Jeena looked at Rallen and grinned. "Oh, he's a terrible influence, there's no doubt about that. So, do we get our three clearances?"

There was a pause. Then: "You're lucky three landing bays just happen to be open right now."

Rallen brought the ship in at least as smoothly as any other he'd ever handled. It felt like he and the ancient ship understood each other.

The first thing they saw when their feet hit the deck was Maxx. The crusty chief mechanic's face was white, and her mouth hung open. Alarmed, Jeena rushed over. "Maxx? You okay?"

Maxx just kept looking at the ship. Eventually, the color began to come back to her face—until it was bright red. "What . . . is . . . *that*?" she yelled.

"We were hoping you'd tell us," Rallen said. "We're late for a meeting with Commander Grant. But go ahead and take a look around, if you want."

Maxx finally took her eyes off the ship in order to glare at Rallen. "I do believe I'll do just that," she said, her anger turning to joy. "Don't hurry back, flyboy. This here baby and me will be just fine without you. Won't we, sweetheart?" she asked, running her hand along the ship.

Rallen and Jeena rushed into Commander Grant's office. They were surprised to see Aldous there as well.

"Sir!" Rallen and Jeena said in unison, snapping to attention.

"At ease," Commander Grant replied. "Sounds like you two have had quite a busy day. Good job. I have something for you," he said, turning away to pick something up from the desk behind him. He handed it to Rallen.

"What's this, sir?" said Rallen, inspecting it.

"It's the latest jetpack the labs have come up with. it's still in its experimental stage, so be careful. And," he added, with a twinkle in his eye, "it's highly unlikely to be any more dangerous than what you've just been through."

Jeena smiled and turned to Rallen. To her amazement, he seemed to be blushing. He quickly turned and pretended to be inspecting the jetpack again.

Commander Grant reached back to the desk and grabbed a few metallic spheres that were lying neatly in a pile. "I thought these might come in handy as well, next time you encounter the Krawl," he said, handing Rallen the spheres. When Rallen held them they felt like gel.

"Whoa!" he cried, grabbing for the spheres as they slipped out of his hands and almost crashed to the floor.

"Easy, Rallen," Commander Grant said, becoming nervous. "Those are the newest combat grenades to come out of the NPP test lab. They act like smart bombs. When thrown, they immediately target the nearest enemy. But they also act like sticky bombs. When in range, the bombs stick to the enemy and can't be removed."

"Then what?" Rallen asked.

"Once in place, they . . . well, you'll see." Grant grinned and nodded to Aldous.

Aldous cleared his throat. "I have something for you as well." He held out a cube. "This is another weapon for the Spectrobe Master."

"Is this my birthday and someone forgot to tell me?" Rallen said, grabbing the cube from Aldous. "What's this do?"

"It creates a force field around whoever wears the Prizmod—a shield, if you will," Aldous replied in his melodramatic manner. "I foresee you requiring it sooner than you'd like. Dark forces—"

He was interrupted by the blaring of an alert siren. Commander Grant accessed the NPP's main computer system. "Speaking of, the Krawl have been spotted heading in the direction of planet Ziba."

"No problem," said Rallen, casually tossing the cube in the air and catching it.

"Problem," corrected Jeena. "Sir, Ziba possesses a strong magnetic field. Any of our ships can make the trip easily enough, but the magnetic field makes precision steering exceedingly difficult. Normally, that's not much of an issue, but if we get into any sort of dogfight or need to adjust course suddenly . . ." Jeena trailed off, then held up a hand, anticipating Rallen's interruption. "Yes, Rallen, it'll even be a problem for a pilot as brilliant as you."

Rallen grinned. "Brilliant, huh? Nice of you to notice at least."

Jeena was about to reply when she noticed Commander Grant lock eyes with Aldous. The old man nodded, and the commander turned back. "Take the new ship."

"Sir?" Jeena said.

"I do not believe it will have the same sort of

issues with the magnetic field as any of our ships would," the commanding officer replied.

"But Commander Grant, we don't know the ship well enough yet. Shouldn't we—" Jeena protested.

Commander Grant held up a hand. "I believe you can trust me on this one. We have uncovered some information regarding the Ancients and the ship. I believe this will be the best course of action."

Jeena snapped to attention, and a second later Rallen did the same. "Yes, sir," they both said.

Professor Kate stepped forward. "If Commander Grant doesn't mind, I'd like to stay at HQ and collaborate with their scientists and see what new information they have on the Ancients."

Grant nodded. "That is more than fine. I am scheduling a major meeting with the entire NPP regarding this new threat once Rallen and Jeena return. I'm sure your input will be more than helpful." He then turned to the two officers. "Is there anything you two would like to ask?"

Rallen hesitated, then said, "Yes, sir. My suit . . . the Prizmod fits into it perfectly, as though it were designed for it. But that's not possible. Is it?"

Commander Grant fell silent, then proceeded. "There is much you will need to know. About the suit, the Spectrobes . . . and the Krawl. But not yet."

He paused, then said abruptly, "Dismissed."

Rallen and Jeena turned and raced out the door.

Grant watched them go, then whispered. "It's happening . . . again . . ."

Chapter Ten

Maxx was not happy. She was just about to investigate the interior of the ancient craft when she was told that it would have to wait.

"Aw, come on," she complained. "Already?"

Rallen was already inside the ship. "Sorry, Maxx," Jeena replied. "Orders. She good to go?"

Maxx threw up her hands in exasperation. "How should I know? Brand-new ship—huge, like nothing I have ever seen before—how do I know if she's space-ready or not?"

Jeena tilted her head. "*Ma-aax*," she sang softly.

Maxx waved Jeena off. "Feh. Yeah, she's good to go. You just better bring her back, you got that? To me—not to anyone else. You hear?"

Jeena pointed at the mechanic. "You and no one else." She smiled. "I promise we'll try not to get hurt, just to make sure you get to check out the ship again."

Maxx turned and walked away. "I don't care whether you get hurt or not, as long as the ship comes back."

As Jeena strapped herself in, Rallen lifted Ancient One into the air.

"How's she handling?" Jeena asked as they broke the atmosphere.

Rallen nodded. "Beautifully. It's weird, she's got so much power—way more than anything I've ever flown." He looked uncharacteristically frustrated. "It's hard to explain. Here, give it a go and you'll see what I mean."

Jeena blinked. "Really?" Most pilots guarded their flight time zealously. And yet here he was handing off control of *this* ship.

It wasn't hard for Rallen to tell what his partner was thinking. "I know," he admitted. "But this is a special situation. There's a good chance you're gonna need to be able to fly this baby. Both our skins might depend upon it."

"Well," Jeena teased as she took control, "aren't *you* getting good at sharing your toys."

Rallen laughed. "That's me. Ah, if only Mom could see me now."

Jeena began to reply, then paused when she saw a haunted look cross Rallen's eyes. She turned away, wanting to respect his privacy, then changed her mind. "What's wrong?"

"Nothing, really." Rallen shrugged. "I just . . ." He paused, then reconsidered. "I just can't help but think about everyone back home. I think 'what if we can't stop the Krawl.' I just want everyone to be safe."

A silence fell over the ship, broken only by the occasional snuffling coming from Komainu.

"Well," Jeena said, "I think you're doing a great job of keeping them, *and* me, safe."

Rallen looked at her from the corner of his eye. "Really?"

Jeena laughed softly. "Yes, Rallen. You're the only person right now that I think can make this all better . . . and . . ." She fell silent, then changed the subject. "So, you were right—this *does* handle perfectly. It's like a really powerful but light-weight scalpel."

"Yes!" Rallen yelled. "Yes! That's it exactly."

Jeena smiled. "So, we got a game plan or what?"

"I don't. I mean, beyond the obvious: find 'em, hit 'em hard, and hit 'em fast."

"Well, it's worked well so far, right?" she agreed.

Turning to Jeena, Rallen gave her a quick wink. "And it may just work again. Check it out—Krawl off the port bow."

"I see them. Multiple vortices," Jeena confirmed.

"What do we know about the planet?" Rallen asked.

"It's small, and its gravity is unstable, due to the planet's solid-iron core." Grinning, she turned to Rallen. "And it's got Krawl on it. Lots of Krawl."

Rallen rubbed his hands together. "Sounds like our kind of planet."

He assumed control of the ship again and hit Ziba's atmosphere. Jeena had said the planet's gravitational pull would be unusually unstable, yet the ship didn't appear to have the least trouble with it.

Rallen banked the ship and began to circle the Krawl from a distance. "Okay," he said. "Looks like it's just the five of them."

"Just?"

"Hey, what can I say? I'm good, remember. Or, rather, *we're* good. Right, guys?" Rallen said, turning to the Spectrobes, who were ready for battle.

Rallen looked closely at Spikanor. He wondered if he was imagining it, or if it was something that came along with being a Spectrobe Master, but he thought he could sense something a little off with the Spectrobe. "Hey—you up for this?"

The Spectrobe turned to look at Rallen and let out a monstrous growl. Rallen put his hands up. "Okay, okay. Sorry I asked."

He turned to Jeena. "Got the ship again?"

"If I need to. What are you thinking?"

Rallen moved toward the back. "I'm thinking it's time to see what this new jetpack can do. Bring us down to just off the deck, if you don't mind."

He jumped clear of the ship. Without

hesitation, the Spectrobes all jumped with him.

Rallen thought he'd have plenty of time to activate the jetpack, but Jeena had been right, Ziba's gravity was *powerful*. He began to plummet faster than he'd imagined possible. Rallen felt so heavy he could barely move his arms. He managed to thumb the jetpack's controls, and his downward momentum was instantly arrested. In fact, he started gaining altitude. Too much altitude.

"This is going to take some getting used to," he muttered.

"Well," came Jeena's voice in his ear, "who better than a Spectrobe Master!"

Rallen slowly decreased the jetpack's propulsion, coming to a gentle landing. "Hey, I'm getting the hang of this," he said. He cut the power completely and immediately was pulled to his knees. "Jeez, you weren't kidding about the gravity down here. I feel like I weigh twice as much!"

"That's because you do," she responded. "Ziba's not big, but its gravitational pull is strong."

Rallen stood and took a step. Okay, he said to himself. I can do this.

He looked up and saw a half-dozen Krawl approaching. "I better be able to do this," he muttered.

These Krawl didn't look anything like the ones on the lava planet of Genshi. They looked like blobs—big, scary, dangerous blobs. They were black and silver; they still had tentaclelike arms, but their hands resembled anvils. And their mouths had huge, sharp, spiked teeth. As unusual as they might appear, there was no mistaking how deadly they were.

The Spectrobes gathered in a semicircle around Rallen: Zozanero on his left, Spikanor on his right, and Danapix directly in front of him. "Here we go. *Iku ze*!" Rallen shouted.

The Spectrobes rushed forward, the two on

his flanks peeled off to the side and Danapix attacked the Krawl directly in front of them.

Rallen attempted to engage one of the Krawl, but moving on Ziba was like trying to run through quicksand. "This gravity is going to be a serious problem," he muttered.

If he couldn't fight the Krawl the way he was accustomed to, it occurred to him, he needed to try something different. Maybe something *really* different. He looked around. The landscape was dotted with high, steep hills. There was no chance he could ever climb one, not with this gravity. Fortunately, he didn't need to.

He fired up his jetpack and flew to the top of the nearest hill. "Yo, tall and ugly!" he called. "Come and get me!"

All three Krawl began moving toward him. "There you go," Rallen called encouragingly. "Keep climbing."

He inserted the cube Aldous had given him

into the Prizmod. "Now, let's see how this bad boy works."

To his delight, he found himself holding a virtual shield. It acted almost like a small force field. "Oh, yeah!" he yelled. "That's what I'm talkin' about. I just hope you're as tough as my laser sword. I guess we'll just have to find out."

Holding the shield with one hand and the laser sword with the other, Rallen hopped forward just a tiny bit. But it was enough.

He slammed into the Krawl, scattering two with his shield and slicing a third in half with his laser sword. The first two tumbled to the bottom of the hill with so much momentum that their upper bodies were driven into the ground, and they were unable to rise. A moment later, both had been taken care of.

Just when Rallen thought he had a second to breathe, two more Krawl were already launching in his direction. "You're gonna have to get me first!" Rallen cried, turning his jetpack to maximum speed. As he blasted up the side of another mountain, the Krawl started gaining momentum. He could feel the anvil-like objects at the ends of their tentacles repeatedly smashing down behind him, coming closer and closer to his jetpack.

"Man, if they hit this pack, I'm done for! Gotta move!" he nervously said to himself.

As Rallen dodged left and right trying to lose the Krawl, they darted left and right with him as if they were learning his patterns.

"Those Krawl are smart!" Jeena's voice said over Rallen's wrist communicator.

"Wait a sec. Smart! That's it! Jeena, you're a genius!" he replied.

Back in Ancient One, Jeena blushed. "Well, I know—but it's all about you right now!"

Rallen grinned as he pulled out two smart bombs he had stored on his belt. "Let's see how smart these Krawl are when they get a load of these little fellas!" He threw two smart bombs straight into the air. They immediately shot back, attached to the Krawl's torsos, and began to glow green. The Krawl looked down, but that's as far as it got. Rallen could hear the explosion behind him and saw pieces of Krawl falling all around him.

"Whoa! Now that's smart!" Turning to face the remaining Krawl, Rallen was blindsided by a flailing tentacle and knocked to the ground.

The Krawl was already a few feet from Rallen, and it's hammerlike arms were right above his head. As Rallen braced for the blow, Zozanero's unmistakable roar blared as he speared the Krawl, sending it crashing to the ground. Zozanero let out another monsterous roar. But his celebration was cut short. Another Krawl came out of nowhere and smashed its metallic tentacle into Zozanero with hurricane force. The Spectrobe flew through the air and crashed into the hard terrain. He let out a painful cry before disappearing into the Prizmod.

"Zozanero?" Rallen cried as he held the Prizmod to his ear. "You okay, buddy?" Rallen's face grew intense. "No one, and I mean no one, hurts my friends! *Iku ze!*"

His laser sword in one hand and the virtual shield in the other, Rallen leaped toward the Krawl, slicing at its tentacles. It soon dissolved into a lifeless puddle of ooze, but as soon as it was gone, three more began making their way toward Rallen.

"Bring it!" Rallen yelled. He turned to Spikanor who had just finished off a Krawl himself. "Spikanor! *Attack*!" With the speed of a hungry lion, Spikanor pounced on the onrushing Krawl, hammering two with his spiked tail and destroying a third with his razor-sharp claws. But a fourth Krawl immediately attacked. This Krawl had a metallic battering ram on its head. It rushed Spikanor like a rhino, hitting him dead on and sending the Spectrobe crashing into the side of a nearby hill. Spikanor slowly limped in Rallen's direction—a Spectrobe never leaves his master.

Suddenly a Krawl swooped down and crashed into the ground alongside Rallen. This Krawl was unlike any Rallen had ever seen. It was twice as big as any of the others—and twice as ferocious. It had multiple heads, two tails, razor-sharp teeth, and dark purple spikes running down its back. Rallen had to look up to see the full array of this massive Krawl. "*You are one . . . big—*"

Rallen didn't get a chance to finish. The Krawl crashed down one of its malletlike tails right where Rallen was standing, barely missing him. Several other Krawl moved out from behind the larger one and made their way toward Rallen and the injured Spectrobe. Behind Rallen, Danapix, was growling, waiting for his master's command.

"Attack!"

Danapix went in for the kill, taking out two Krawl with a lightning attack that sent them both flying back straight into a distant mountain. Before Danapix could release another blast, Rallen saw the larger Krawl making its way to Spikanor.

"Danapix!" Rallen cried. "Protect Spikanor!" The Spectrobe nodded and leaped directly in front of Spikanor, letting out a roar that could be heard for miles.

"This doesn't look good, Jeena," Rallen yelled into his wrist communicator.

"Rallen! Get back to the ship! You can't face all of them! Especially that big one!"

Rallen knew she was right, but he

wasn't one to retreat, even though he knew the odds were against him. Spikanor was down and Danapix was now surrounded by several Krawl, with the largest one right in front of him. Rallen got a cold chill down his spine. He knew the end might be near for him and his friends.

Then suddenly, his Prizmod grew bright and a humming sound could be heard coming from within it. He knew just what that meant.

"Well. Looks like someone has Evolved!" Rallen held up his Prizmod to the sky. *"Iku ze!"*

A beam of light cascaded up into the night sky, and out came Aoba. He flew through the air, leaving a trail of fire in his wake. Aoba screeched loudly as he swooped down to grab the Krawl with his massive claws, carrying them into the distance and dropping them to the iron-covered ground where they shattered into a thousand pieces. Aoba landed next to Danapix, and they turned to each other. It looked as if they were nodding in unison. Then they headed straight for each other with great velocity. When the two Spectrobes collided, a blinding light shot out from where they stood. This electric pulse slammed into the largest Krawl, decimating it on impact. When the smoke cleared, the two Spectrobes stood unharmed, ready for another battle. As for the massive Krawl, not a smidgeon of dust was left of it. All three Spectrobes returned to the Prizmod without a sound, and the night air was suddenly quiet.

Rallen fell to his knees from exhaustion. "Whoa."

"Hey, did you see what I just saw?" Jeena said over the comm.

"I had front-row seats," Rallen said.

"You about ready to go home?" Jeena asked.

"Am I ever," he responded.

"Come on, let's get out of here. I'm tired and hungry . . . and you just know what tomorrow will probably bring."

"Even more Krawl?" Jeena questioned.

"Even more Krawl."

Chapter Eleven

"Jado. Come."

The High Krawl stepped forward.

"What have you to say for yourself?"

Jado replied softly, "I am sorry I did not fulfill my mission on Genshi."

"Mmm. That is one way of putting it. I am not happy, Jado. Perhaps you are not to be trusted with such an assignment in the future. Perhaps we should consider . . . alternate fates for you."

"No," Jado said, adding with some difficulty,

"Please. Give me another chance. The Spectrobe Master and his partner are young and new. I will make sure they do not live long enough to gain the necessary experience."

"Young and new. Yes, they are. And yet you were unable to defeat them. Your arrogance may be your downfall yet."

Jado did not reply.

"But perhaps . . . yes, perhaps I shall give you another chance." The dark figure reached into his cloak and pulled out a fossilized Spectrobe. "Take this. Expose it to the Krawl source and you will have—"

"A Dark Spectrobe? But how can I—"

"Do not question me!" The shadowy figure hissed. "Do as I say, and you will be redeemed. Fail again . . ."

"I shall not fail again, Master Krux. The Spectrobes and their human master shall be destroyed."